OPPOSITES

Carol Watson
Illustrated by David Higham
Consultant: Betty Root
Tutor-in-Charge, Centre for the Teaching of Reading,
University of Reading.

Tom and Henry are friends.

Tom is **fat**.

Henry is **thin.**

They have two dogs called Sam
and Scrap.

Sam has **long** legs,

but Scrap's legs are **short**.

Sam lives in a **big** kennel.

Scrap's kennel is **small**.

Tom's house is at the **bottom** of a hill.

Henry's house is at the **top**.

One day Henry and Tom
go for a drive.

Henry has an **old** car,

but Tom's car is **new**.

They go **up** a hill

and **down** a hill.

At first the road is **wide**.

Then it is **narrow.**

They go **under** one bridge

and **over** another bridge.

Tom drives too fast near the river.
He falls **in**.

Henry pulls him **out**.

Tom is **wet**,

but Henry is **dry.**

Tom feels very **sad**,

but soon he feels **happy** again.

Puzzle picture
How many opposites can you find in the picture below?

First published in 1983
Usborne Publishing Ltd
20 Garrick St London
WC2 9BJ, England
© Usborne Publishing Ltd 1983

The name of Usborne and the
device 🎈 are Trade Marks of
Usborne Publishing Ltd.
Printed in Belgium by Casterman S.A.